MA

MALVERN

D0297724

JUNIOR

Please return/renew this item by the last date shown

worcestershire
c o u n t y c o u n c i l
Libraries & Learning

700036622692

OUR DAFT DOG
DANNY

VIKING

Published by the Penguin Group
Penguin Group (Australia)
250 Camberwell Road
Camberwell, Victoria 3124, Australia
(a division of Pearson Australia Group Pty Ltd)
Penguin Group (USA) Inc.
375 Hudson Street, New York, New York 10014, USA
Penguin Group (Canada)
90 Eglinton Avenue East, Suite 700,
Toronto ON M4P 2Y3, Canada
(a division of Pearson Penguin Canada Inc.)
Penguin Books Ltd
80 Strand, London WC2R 0RL, England
Penguin Ireland
25 St Stephen's Green, Dublin 2, Ireland
(a division of Penguin Books Ltd)
Penguin Books India Pvt Ltd
11, Community Centre, Panchsheel Park, New Delhi-110 017, India
Penguin Group (NZ)
67 Apollo Drive, Rosedale, North Shore 0632, New Zealand
(a division of Pearson New Zealand Ltd)
Penguin Books (South Africa) (Pty) Ltd
24 Sturdee Avenue, Rosebank, Johannesburg 2196, South Africa

Penguin Books Ltd, Registered Offices: 80 Strand, London WC2R 0RL, England

First published by Penguin Group (Australia), 2009

10 9 8 7 6 5 4 3 2

Text and illustrations copyright © Pamela Allen, 2009

The moral right of the author and illustrator has been asserted.

All rights reserved. Without limiting the rights under copyright reserved above,
no part of this publication may be reproduced, stored in or introduced into a retrieval
system, or transmitted, in any form or by any means (electronic, mechanical, photocopying,
recording or otherwise), without the prior written permission of both the copyright
owner and the above publisher of this book.

Design by Deborah Brash © Penguin Group (Australia)
Typeset in 21 pt Delicato
Colour reproduction by Splitting Image, Clayton, Victoria
Made and printed in China by Everbest Printing Co. Ltd

National Library of Australia
Cataloguing-in-Publication data:

   Allen, Pamela.
   Our daft dog Danny

   ISBN 978 0 670 07335 1

   Dogs-Juvenile fiction.

A823.3

puffin.com.au

OUR DAFT DOG
DANNY

Pamela Allen

PENGUIN|VIKING

To Thomas, Toby and Aria

Uncle Peter's house is in the sandhills by the beach.
He lives there with his dog Millie.
We love to visit them,
even in winter when it's cold.

Then we roll up our trousers
and chase the waves.

Uncle Peter throws the ball for Millie.
He can throw a long, long way.

Millie always catches it and brings it back.

Today for the first time we have
brought our dog Danny with us.
Danny loves the beach too.

But when Uncle Peter threw the ball,
Danny chased Millie and grabbed her tail.

Millie howled
and howled
but Danny wouldn't let go.

Poor Millie.
She yanked and she yelped.
She bounced and she barked.
She snarled and she snapped.

But Danny wouldn't let go.

Uncle Peter shouted,
'Stop it! Naughty dog! Let go!'

We pulled and pulled but still
Danny wouldn't let go.
Poor Millie!

When Danny got tired and did at last let go,
Uncle Peter was cross.

'We're going home,' he growled.
'And don't bring THAT DAFT DOG
with you ever again.'

At home we were miserable. We all wanted
the beach to be fun, even Uncle Peter.
What could we do?

It was Uncle Peter who reached up high and
took down a jar of 'Geoff's Hot Chilli Sauce'
from the top shelf of the kitchen cupboard.
'This should fix things,' he said. 'Come on.'

And we set off for the beach again.
Uncle Peter held out Millie's tail,
I held the jar and Toby smeared the sauce —
up and down and round and round.

When Millie's tail was completely covered
in hot chilli sauce, Uncle Peter threw the ball.

Millie chased it and . . .

EEEEOW – YUK!

'Yuk! Yuk! Yuk!' yowled Danny.

'He won't do that again,' said Toby.
We took the howling Danny home for
a drink of water. We felt sorry for him.
We'd spoilt his game and he was miserable.
We wanted Danny to have fun at the beach too.

What could we do?

In the garden shed we found some rope.

Toby gave the rope to Uncle Peter.
'What's this for?' he asked.

'Wait and see,' I said. 'It's Toby's good idea. Come on.'

Then off we went to the beach again.

When Uncle Peter saw our new game,

Then he threw the ball . . .

he laughed. 'Clever boy, Toby.'

a long, long way.

Danny grabbed the pretend tail.

'Look! It's a tug-o-war,'
yelled Toby. 'Come on.'

Sometimes we won.

Sometimes Danny won.

And sometimes nobody won.

But it didn't matter, because now
the beach was fun again for all of us.

On the way home, Toby asked,
'Can we bring Danny with us next time we come?'

What do *you* think Uncle Peter said?